For Karen and Brian
– L J

For David and Jane
– C W

Published in 1996 by
Magi Publications
22 Manchester Street, London W1M 5PG

Text © 1996 Linda Jennings
Illustrations © 1996 Catherine Walters

Printed and bound in Belgium by
Proost N.V., Turnhout

ISBN 1 85430 395 3

COME BACK,
BUSTER

by Linda Jennings

illustrated by Catherine Walters

Buster was a small dog with a black patch over one eye.
He lived with Mr Merrydew, who had taken him in when
he was homeless. Buster loved his new friend and his home,
and the visits from Mr Merrydew's grandchildren, Jake,
Becky and Rose.

The children were lively and noisy. They gave Buster lots
of doggy sweets, and Mr Merrydew would take them all for
lovely walks in the park.

One day, when Jake fetched Buster's lead as usual,
Mr Merrydew shook his head.
"Sorry, children," he said. "No walk in the park today.
My old heart's playing up a bit. Give Buster a run round
the garden instead."

After that Mr Merrydew took Buster only for very short
walks, but Buster didn't mind. He was happy enough just
living quietly at home with his old friend.

Then suddenly everything changed.
One cold blustery day in October, Buster woke up,
feeling uneasy. Why hadn't Mr Merrydew come
downstairs for breakfast? Buster whined and scratched
at the kitchen door, but, though he could hear
Mr Merrydew's faint voice from upstairs, the old man
did not come.

Later that morning Mr Merrydew's daughter, Mary,
arrived, and gave Buster his breakfast. Buster wondered
what was going on. There were a lot of comings and
goings in the house, and a big white van with a red cross
drew up outside the gate. He sat on the doorstep,
wondering what would happen next.

Suddenly Buster heard Mr Merrydew's bedroom door open.
He saw two people carrying his old friend down the stairs
on a stretcher.

"Goodbye, Buster," said Mr Merrydew faintly, as he
raised a trembling hand. But before Buster could
lick it, the stretcher was carried outside to the
white van, and Mr Merrydew wasn't there
any more.

Buster ran out into the garden. Where
was his old friend going?

Mary caught hold of Buster's collar, and took him indoors.
She picked up his basket and his toys and his dog bowl,
and clipped on his lead.

"Everything will be all right, Buster," she said.

"You're coming back home with me."

Mary tried to lead Buster towards the car, but he drew back.

Once, long ago, some cruel people had put him in a car,
and thrown him out into the cold wintry night.

Surely Mary wouldn't do that?

Mary was stronger than Buster. She picked him up easily,
put him in the back, where there was a nice large space
for him, and drove off.

The journey seemed long, because Buster was
frightened, but it was only to the other side
of town. At last the car swung into a driveway,
and Mary opened the car door.
"It's Buster!" the children shouted as they
rushed out of the house. "But where's Grandad?"
"Grandad's gone to hospital," explained Mary.
"He's had a small heart attack, and we're going to
look after Buster for him."
The children looked sad, but soon cheered up.
"Can we take Buster for a walk?" asked Rose,
tugging at his lead.
But Buster was still scared, and the children
were making too much noise.

Buster wriggled and pulled, and pulled and wriggled,
till his collar came off. Before anyone could stop him,
he was off down the drive and out of the gate.
His only thought was to run back to his own home,
where things were quiet and cosy, and never changed.

Though Buster had never been out alone in this part
of town, somehow he knew his way home.
Through a busy market he ran, with people rushing by,
and shouting at him. Once, long ago, when he had been
a little stray dog, angry voices had shouted like that.
But on he raced, hoping that the way would lead him
back to Mr Merrydew.

At long last Buster came to the very park where Mr Merrydew and the children had once taken him for walks. He ran through the playground and down to the pond, just in case Mr Merrydew was there on his favourite bench. But he wasn't, and Buster sat down sadly.

Before Buster had the chance to rest, a big fierce dog
ran up to him, growling.
"Get lost, you mongrel!" he barked, and ran after Buster,
snapping and snarling, as far as the park gates.

Buster's paws were sore, and he felt very tired and hungry.
So much had happened to him that day. But right there
ahead of him Buster could see his old home, and he ran up
to it happily. The gate was shut, so he jumped over
the low garden wall.

The house looked cold and empty.
Buster scratched at the door to be let in,
but nobody opened it. He ran round to the
back, and looked through the french windows.
There was no fire in the grate, and no tea on
the table.
And then Buster knew that Mr Merrydew was
not there at all.

Buster sat down on the cold step, and thought
of the loud cheerful children, with their warm
hugs and the endless little treats they gave him.
He thought of the long walks, and the wild
chases across the park.
But, though he had found his way to his own
home, he could not remember how to get
back to the children again.

A car drew up at the gate, and Buster ran into the shadow of the hedge. He was still frightened of cars.

"Buster! Buster!" called three worried voices.

"Are you there, Buster?"

It was the children!

Buster crawled out, his tail wagging for the first time that day. Jake picked him up, and hugged him. Buster felt warm in his arms.

"You're coming home with us," cried Rose, and she gave him a crunchy chocolate biscuit.

Buster never ran away again, though he still missed Mr Merrydew.

Then one day, just before Christmas, he had a wonderful surprise . . .

. . . the door opened,
and in came his old friend!
"Buster!" cried Mr Merrydew, with tears
in his eyes, as he gathered the little dog into
his arms.
"Grandad's coming to live with us!" said
Becky. "Won't that be great?"
Of course it would, thought Buster.
It would be the best Christmas present ever!
"Woof!" he said, his little stumpy tail
wagging nineteen to the dozen.